Karen grew up in a small town in north-eastern Victoria, Australia where she rode horses through a beautiful landscape of eucalypts, lakes, and snow-capped mountains. Her love of country continues to influence both her fiction and nonfiction writing. She built a career in a range of educational settings culminating in heading Australia's first writing and publishing degree. She holds a Ph.D. and M.Ed. (Hons) in the areas of myth and fantasy as well as a range of post-graduate qualifications in Education, ESL, and Literacy. Karen travels extensively overseas but enjoys nothing more than camping in the Australian Outback.

Glastonbury - Meditations on the Goddess is Karen's third book to use poetry to explore the power of journeying. She is also the author of 17 fantasy novels. She lives in Melbourne and writes full time. You can find out more about Karen and her books on her website.

Connect with K.S. Nikakis

Amazon: https://www.amazon.com/author/ksnikakis
Twitter: https://twitter.com/KSNikakis
Facebook: www.facebook.com/ksnikakis
Goodreads: www.goodreads.com
Website: www.ksnikakis.com
Email: author@ksnikakis.com

WORKS BY K S NIKAKIS

Non Fiction
Travel and Poetry

Journey: Seeking the Sacred, Spirit and Soul
in the Australian Wilderness
In the Company of Birds: Poems from an
Outback Odyssey
Glastonbury - Meditations on the Goddess

Fantasy Novels
Series

Angel Caste series:
Angel Blood
Angel Breath
Angel Bone
Angel Bound
Angel Blessed
Angel Caste – Complete 5 Book Series

The Kira Chronicles trilogy:*
The Whisper of Leaves
The Song of the Silvercades
The Cry of the Marwing
remnant hard copies only

The Kira Chronicles series:
The Whisper of Leaves
The Silence of Stone
The Secrets of Stars
The Thunder of Hoofs
The Crying of Birds

The Music of Home
The Kira Chronicles – Complete 6 Book Series

Fantasy Novels

The Emerald Serpent
Heart Hunter
The Third Moon
Messenger
I Heard the Wolf Call My Name – *Finalist -
Best YA Novel Aurealis Awards, 2019*

Fantasy Novels – YA

The Dragon of the Drowned World

Fantasy Short Stories

The White Stag and Other Stories – With Deep Fantasy
Retellings
including
Glass-Heart – Finalist –
Best YA Short Story Aurealis Awards, 2019

Glastonbury Meditations on the Goddess

K.S. NIKAKIS

First published by SOV CONSULTING LLC - SOV Media Australia 2025 Amazon: www.amazon.com.au

Glastonbury Meditations on the Goddess
© copyright by KS Nikakis 2025

Publisher: SOV CONSULTING LLC - SOV Media Melbourne, Australia.

Cover: C Nikakis
Image: K.S. Nikakis
Typography: Adobe Brushscript; Benguiat Std.

National Library of Australia
Cataloguing-in-Publication entry: Nikakis, Karen Simpson

Glastonbury Meditations on the Goddess
ISBN 978-0-6451927-5-9

For the Goddess in all of us

Contents

Glastonbury – Meditations on the Goddess. 1
Prologue. 1
Portals 3
Triple Form Goddess 5
Time. 7
Temples 9
Names 12
Travellers 15
Cemeteries 18
Metamorphisis 21
Labrynths 23
Holy Water 25
Epilogue. 27
Works by Karen Simpson Nikakis 30

GLASTONBURY
MEDITATIONS ON THE GODDESS

Prologue

I first visited Glastonbury Abbey's ruins 46 years ago. It was a freezing, iron-grey day in January, with winter-black trees clad in a hoar-frost so thick it resembled blossom. Being deep in winter, the site was deserted and it is cold once more on this, my second visit (November 2024). The sky is the same flat grey and again, there are few other people around, making me grateful for the silence and space to fully take in this sacred space.

On my first visit in 1978, mist streamered between the Abbey's soaring arches and time seemed so odd I half expected Merlin to appear between the stones. This visit shares the same sense of other-worldly glamor despite the lack of mist. The Abbey is strewn with the last golden leaves of autumn which, in their glow against the grey, seem just as magical.

On this trip, I have time to explore the town of Glastonbury but for some odd reason, had ruled out returning to the Abbey ruins. Perhaps I was fearful of destroying the mystical memories of my first visit, but on my very last day in Glastonbury, I change my mind and am so glad I did.

Of course, there is far more to Glastonbury than the Abbey ruins or the famous music festival. It was a sacred space long before Christianity claimed it and continues to be so. Many of Glastonbury's sacred sites are mapped and marketed but others have been lost, along with those who once knew them. Yet they remain, sometimes hidden, sometimes in plain sight, for those with a willingness to see.

Finding them requires a casting aside of judgement and an openness to the infiniteness of possibility which means a preparedness to look, and listen, and reflect. The sacred might dwell in a toss of leaves or a strew of pinecones; a subtle glimmer of still water or a spring's transient bubbles; a moss-marked grave or the grinning gargoyle perched above it. And as I slowly explore Glastonbury, I find the sacred in many places and no doubt miss it in others.

I call these glimpses of the sacred the Goddess, for if there is one great, omniscient creator spirit, then surely it must be a She for, despite what countless godmen have claimed over the centuries, life always has and always will flow from the feminine.

Portals

However the sacred manifests, we must navigate a portal to take us from the conscious here and now, to the unconscious other, the domain of myth and dream, archetype and symbol, and ultimately, of the Goddess.

Alice through the looking-glass
Alice down the rabbit hole
the missteps of hapless travellers over misty moors
the ill-judged peerings of the curious through keyhole portals
into the halls of faerie dance

The long slumbers of Snow White, Sleeping Beauty, and Rip Van Winkle
are portals too
and the grander ones of once-and-future Kings
ensconced in their lonely mountain caves
endlessly waiting for their time
to come around again

The break between the here and now
is seldom pleasant however it comes
a branch storm-torn
or slow-eaten by rot
must fall
and leave behind a world
full of certainties

Arrival in the other is a different matter entirely
cast upon alien shores

loath to pay the ferryman
we are all kings
over-thinking
under-acting
at rest on our stone beds
but never rested

Marooned between portals
exits and entries
doors with ornate black hinges, mullions, and tympana
adorned with demons and gods
keyed by arcane verses
or by magic
or in humbler beast-dug burrows, dung-strewn
garlanded with autumn leaves long spent
no gayness of gold here, no harbingers of brighter futures
just sludge but potent never-the-less
for those with eyes to see
and wits to follow

Down, down we go for the journey is always down
away from the bright lights of logic
from the neat illuminations of the rational
from the comforting snug of the familiar
into the stinking morass into which all things sink
that yearn to be reborn

Nothing escapes unchanged
the dissolution subtle or shocking
but always absolute

Triple-Form Goddess

The Triple-Form Goddess (the nymph/maiden, matron/ mother, and crone) is less well known than the male duality of the hero and wise, old man, but far older than the Christian trinity of the Father, Son, and Holy Ghost. The Goddess is many parts yet one, ever-changing but always the Goddess. The metamorphosis from girl to mother, and mother to wisewoman, is shared by millions of women, regardless of time and place but rarely recognised or valued.

In contemporary culture, women are exhorted to retain their youthful beauty but I was glad to trade my ignorant blonde attractiveness for the wisdom of a lined, silver-haired crone, and celebrated my transition with a triskele tattoo in acknowledgement of the Triple-Form Goddess.

In the depths of our unconscious
we leave behind the masculine world and join the feminine
for life and death are women's work:
cradling the bloodied newborn's squirm
cleaning the cooling corpse

It is feminine magic that rules here
though rule belongs to the harder hand of kings
not the guiding one of queens

No cross survives this bog of unbeing, no holy rood with
arms out-stretched
as taut as Christ's more fragile ones
survives a soup so old the world lacked words
to name it

In this fecund mix the Triple-Form Goddess uncurls Herself
like a fern's unfettered fronds
Her parts not fixed by the crucifier's spike but by the heart
the spiritus mundi, anima mundi, femina mundi

making and unmaking
like the peasant who thieves the ruined castle's stones
to build some ruder shelter for himself

The sunny promise of the girl child
running humming through the flower-strewn meadow
gives way to the fleeter-footed Diana
on hunt through some ancient forest
for a mate half worthy of her
and the huntress in turn gives way
to the wizened crone crouched in her mossy cave
watching the world
with eyes as sharp as knives

The crone knows the girl must die as a caterpillar must
to birth a moth
and the moth must egg-lay
or the circle be forever broken
like a crescent moon
never to find its fullness

The moth's swirl around the moon is the same
as its swirl around the candle, lamp, fluorescent bulb
a helix that arcs skywards and earthwards
or a spiral as flat as a toy train's circular track
its revolutions the same and different
separated yet unified by Time

Time

A long haul flight dismantles all notion of Time. The day and time I embark, the clock-shown time of stopovers, the time I arrive, bear no relationship to the days, hours, minutes prior to my departure. I must abandon Time's old rules, as arbitrary as they are, and embrace Time's new ones.

It is November 2024 in the ruined Abbey's grounds, but I stand where I stood 46 years earlier or perhaps only a moment ago. And while I stand there, the unsettling realisation comes to me that while I know a lot about how to measure Time, I know nothing of Time itself.

Time is hard to pin down for all its power
the past filled with haunting horrors
or half-imagined joys
the future filled with dread
or golden promise

Past and future seem imprinted, hard-wired
unlike the present
which is amorphous, fleeting, fragile
like an amoeba that splits itself into past and future
to be forever annihilated
by its ever twinning offspring

Time is easier to grasp in the mountains' deep silence
where it runs on like a gleaming stream
cargoed with leaves, gold and brown
green stuff torn from its bed
and a strange scum of unbeauty
the mirror-backing of

the admired bright

The stream flows away beyond our ken
but there is froth sometimes, the friction drag of the present
that crouches like a lumpish opaque gem
holding fast to the river-bed with ancient, Time-wise claws
sending an alchemy of air and water
to remind us of the ever-moving, ever stilling nature
of Time

Temples

I have long labeled built places of worship temples, whether they be churches, synagogues, mosques or other religious constructions, and the grey stone tower of the temple of St John the Baptist catches my eye on my very first day in Glastonbury.

It fills the window of my Airbnb and is visible from many parts of town. The temple is situated prominently in the High Street and I pass it several times on my way to and from sites I wrongly believe more noteworthy.

So, it is not until the penultimate day of my visit that I step through its iron gates in search of the elusive Glastonbury Thorn and discover so much more.

There are watchers in the stone
perched on holy walls
or sheltered by niches in the narthex and steeple sides
eyes still sharp from the mason's mallet
saints and martyrs, Mary and her son
dumb beasts attendant at some
ancient birth

Other things watch with duller, moss-filled eyes
and lichen-stoppered mouths
unnamed, unknown
unlike the grotesques perched high upon the temple roof
to ward off evil or else to seal it in

Every temple welcomes and rejects
sifts wheat from chaff, friend from stranger

the faithful from the infidel, but all is grist to the Goddess
mill
She grinds them down whoever they are
for they come from Her and to Her
they must return

The grotesques have company
metal-gulleted gargoyles who send the Goddess's rain
far from the godmen's hallowed walls
but grotesques and gargoyles are Her creations too
magicked from deeper, darker places than the sunny hill
of crucifixion
and Her waters fall where She intends
a shining shower to glim the tombs and broken statuary
shelters of the devout and secret doubters
alike

She delivers an endless seep as well
to hasten journeys down through rotting coffins
to Her great cauldron of un-making
the welcome there of corpse and carrion the same
the godly and the godless
joined in one almighty mix

The temple vestibule is webbed with spandrels
to form four stars all held within a fifth
as the Goddess holds all
within Herself

An angel crouches on the wall below
caught between ecclesiastical embellishments
and the humbler flags of stone

It was ever thus this layering

temples built upon some older god-touched ruin
and it, in turn, upon a spring's slow bubble
oak-sheltered
fan-fared not by angel trumpets
but by a fox's rough-tongued lap

Temples insist on more formal hallowings
than the gratitude of thirsty beasts
demanding the god's firm hand
or his form made manifest
flesh-fashioned into chiseled stone,
bloodied mortar to hold it all together
and a mighty tower
in warning to the Goddess

But the Goddess is inured to such intrusions
usurpers come and go like leaves upon the wind
and She Herself is flux
everchanging
sloughing and reskinning Herself like stone
that grinds to dust and is pressed to stone again

Names

Words hold power, not just in communication, but in spells and charms and prayers. Some contemporary cultures rename God and Hell as Gosh and Heck in secular speech, in the same way as historically, the devil was named Old Nick, to avoid the risk of summoning him by voicing his real name.

Nowhere is the power of naming more obvious than in war. Terrorist v. Freedom-fighter, Incursion v. invasion, passive voice rather than active voice used to blunt the horrors of atrocities and obscure blame. The effects of name choices can linger on through the centuries. The 'is' ending of Nikakis, my Cretan name by marriage, is said to have been imposed by the Otterman Turks who ruled Crete for over two hundred years. The 'is' being a diminutive, turned all Cretans into 'little' people under Otterman rule.

Even the reversion of European place names to their First Nation originals in Australia, can elicit furious responses as demonstrated by Ayres Rock (named after the Chief Secretary of South Australia in 1873) being returned to its First Nation name of Uluru. Fraser Island reverting to K'gari is a more recent example.

Temples are named for their protectors
or for the sufferers of brutal, bloody deaths
or for their martyred acolytes

Their faces are fused into leaded windows
to form bright panes of blue and green and ruby red
or cast in plaster icons

and hammered onto temple walls
like Christ was hammered to the cross

The Goddess has no need of names
forged in the fiery mouths of men
incised in stone with barbs and bullets
to be overwritten or erased
by the next all-conquering
god-appointed power

The lost songs of minstrels
and the fading ink on scrolls unwriting
name the Goddess as a tree is named
according to its time and place
or leaves and bark and branches
with no regard for roots or other hidden parts
and so the tree remains a thing of mystery
as the Goddess does

Her name is not the work of men in any case
but the chink of ice slow-crushed
by sluggish streams roused from winter dreams
the scything pulse of birds in uplift to the heavens
the steam of sun-found frost
that hangs
in glittering veils between the worlds
an infant's first sharp breath
and an elder's final frail one

The temple has its servers as the Goddess does
not the slow soil-churn of mole and worm
or the hold-release of water by the forests' roots and leaves
but god-appointed priests to rule the pulpits
carillonneurs to ring the bells

and local worthies (or those in fear of death)
to fill the coffers

But there are other powers here too
unnamed, unnoticed
the dusters and moppers of altars and pews
the bringers of fresh flowers and removers of dead blooms
silver-haired crones in sensible garb
beyond the sexual want of men
beyond the duties of daughter, sister, wife and mother
free at last to walk the Goddess path

Travellers

The longer I spend exploring Glastonbury, the more I sense its timelessness. It's not just knowing that beneath a tarmacked street lies cobbles, and beneath the cobbles lies an ancient trackway rutted by wagons and hard-printed by human feet, but understanding that these streets pass through sacred spaces sustained by our ancestors' yearning (and our own) for that unknowable transcendent beauty beyond our human state.

There are travellers through myth and Time
celebrated, acclaimed then denigrated, dismissed
torn from pedestals, smashed and burned
but never truly lost

History is written by the victors
and myth passed from mouth to mouth
before it finds a quill

Both are prone to error innocent or contrived
yet what the brain finds nonsense
the heart and soul might still insist
on holding close

Once and future kings were here, or so they say
Arthur laid to rest on Avalon's fair isle
but never dead, just sleeping
and the child Jesus arrived on some brief visit
and returned to far off lands to die
upon the cross
and leave behind an empty tomb

His trader uncle did return, or so they say
to thrust his staff in Wearyall Hill's rich soil
to sprout and blossom a hawthorn tree
hacked and burned
to come again (like any once and future king)
a Clootie tree
beribboned with the pilgrims' dreams
hacked and burned a second time
like some half-forgotten martyr

But dreams are not so easily dispatched
the roots of myth run deep, too deep
for the savagery that sweeps the world
in cycles
as regular as storms

The hawthorn buds and flowers
where it will
as the Goddess does
within the temple's shadow
and in the hidden places
and those within plain sight

It gifts its blossoms to queens and kings
more transient than those who wait
in waking sleep
to rule this world again

Other travellers pass this way
shouldered by the grieving
or drawn by black-horsed hearses
or motorised ones
to pause amongst the temple's hymns and prayers
but not to stay

the graveyard heaves with corpses
piled so thick they lap the temple walls
so on they go, these newer dead
to other resting places

Cemeteries

I have wandered the art deco tombs of Paris's famous Pere-Lachaise Cemetery, the mossy grandeur of London's Highgate Cemetery, and the red dust of countless Australian Outback cemeteries where the only company is the stick of flies and the mournful cry of crows.

Cemeteries (and graveyards), wherever located, are places of story and even the briefest of stories incised on headstones reveals that grief is the conjoined twin of love. But cemeteries, in particular, because they tend to be located beyond the hubbub of settlements, are also places of bird call and the hop of small animals which together, seem to celebrate the hope and beauty of life.

Glastonbury Cemetery rolls away in stony swales
determined by faith and fashion
Celtic, Calvary and botonee crosses
headstones graced with lambs and lilies, grapes and vines
broken steles
Christ and the angels, the Goddess in Her Mary form
stalwart vaults and crypts
and mortuary houses
Conformists and Nonconformists set side by side
closer in death than they ever were
in life

Death dismembers every guest
regardless of class and creed
beneath the weed-infested plot or
the mason's grander work
bones are bones, and in the end

just dust
the stuff of some new enterprise
decided by the Goddess

There's a plot here less grave than garden
mounded with plantings, strewn with flowers
single-stemmed like lovers' tokens
or tied in bright bouquets of homage

Dion Fortune took her name from some ancestral motto
coined to justify an affluence gained through guns
Deo, non Fortuna - God, not Luck the guilty party claimed
but Violet Mary Firth seems a far more fitting name
for a spiritualist, occultist, writer and
wielder of ceremonial magic

The Goddess likes to mix things up
violet a blend of red and blue
a firth where the Goddess's sweet waters
mingle with Her salt
and Mary - the Goddess name in lesser form
a distillation to fit this place and Time
but fluid nevertheless
Maria, Maryam, Miriam, Mariam
and Isis before them all

The temple gods confer much grander titles
on the Goddess
Our Lady, Holy Virgin, Madonna, Blessed
Mother, Mother of God
to elevate Her to some lofty pedestal
a fair-skinned virgin, remote and pure
safe from meddling in the god-affairs of men
no hag or crone or woodland witch is welcomed here

to sully the inner sanctum with her steely gaze
and grimy pointing finger

Yet motherhood was never pure
just messy sex and swelling
the bloody pain of birthing
the sweet release of suckling
and the endless mother-fear
that Death will come a calling
and rob the world of joy

On the grassy slopes above the cemetery's stone
beyond a fence of wood and wire
there lies the Green Cemetery
with graves marked out with autumn leaves
watched over by a strong-backed oak
with roots called down through corpse and cleft
to dwell within the Goddess

Metamorphosis

Having the good luck to live to cronehood gifts me the chance to experience, witness, and reflect on change firsthand. While some changes seem abrupt and violent, and others so slow as to be scarcely noticeable, they gradually assume a disturbing similarity to what has gone before. The paradox that 'history teaches us that history teaches us nothing' seems proved and supports the notion that Time, however defined, is a spiral rather than a helix, that endlessly repeats the Past's mistakes.

I find myself hoping that we have the power to pursue an individual helix, regardless of the spiral we were born into, and so alter our trajectories to ones more enlarging and sustaining.

Some godmen deny the Goddess Her slow reclaiming
rearranging, reincarnating
who refuse the saintly and the martyred
their rightful journey through disintegration, re-integration
who insist the dead remain
amongst the living

Arranged along the altar are withered bits of this and that
slabs of skull and finger joints
vials of blood more brown than red

They keep the cross and candles company
and guarantee the temple and its visitors
protection
but nothing is ever safe
temples crouched upon the charred remains of others
may one day face the torch themselves

and the icon's slow procession through the village streets
become a deadly race before the howling mob
even the fate of temple gods remains unclear
for the Goddess owns them too

When memories fail She loans them out
and like a turgid stream's slow circumambulation
it brings them round again
for second viewings

On Beckery's factoried-slopes/Bride's unsullied mound/
Brigid's monkish ruins
(all or none for Time is an origami folded in upon itself)
Arthur met the Goddess in Her Mary guise,
in one century or another, in myth or dream
where Time's crisp creases meet

He traded his dragon for a crystal cross, or so they say
but the dragon was never his to trade
no dragon ever is
and while the cross is lost, as such things are
the dragon still remains
Bride or Mary, the great creator Tiamat
or other serpent/worms who,
despite the godmen's writings,
remain immune from spears

They curl within the deeper, darker
fecund places to guard the Goddess treasure
the mighty cycles of transformation
rot and regeneration
that take us back to Her great belly
and send us forth again

Labyrinths

When I finally visit the temple that honours John the Baptist, I am delighted to discover its grounds contain a labyrinth. I walk it slowly and in silence, as I walk labyrinths wherever I find them. This one is soggy and I later learn, soon to be closed for winter. I barely notice the mud as I enter the meditative state that labyrinths gift and emerge centered, at peace, and feeling closer to the Goddess.

There is no minotaur in the labyrinth
marked out on muddy temple grounds
no wild flight through darkness guided only by a thread
and a lover soon to be discarded

There is no half-man half-beast waiting at the labyrinth's heart
nothing to slay except the monsters in our numinous dreams
mythic, malformed, magnificent
male and female joined, godman and Goddess together
as we all are in our Shadows
perfect in our imperfection

We must gaze upon our ugliness unflinchingly
embrace it and make it ours
not fail the test as Perseus did
who slew Medusa
and turned his heart to stone

Theseus failed as well
abandoned Ariadne/his female part
to rule as warrior kings do
until he too was discarded

tossed into the all encompassing sea
of Jung's unconscious

There is a second labyrinth, or so they say
incised on the Tor's steep shoulders
that leads to the ruined tower
at the labyrinth's heart

The tower survived the lustful king
whose blows smashed temples everywhere
who murdered those who loved him best
and those who stood against him

He martyred godmen here
like Pilate martyred Christ
their blood seeped down
though broken temple timbers
past Roman relics and flints knapped sharp
to Gwyn ap Nudd's domain of death and faerie
down, down to where waters stirred
White Spring and Red Spring
to be gifted back to sunlit soils
in endless rituals of renewal
by the Goddess

Holy Water

The psychoanalyst Carl Jung and the famous mythologer Joseph Campbell both identified the descent underground and the presence of water in myth and dream as archetypes of the unconscious. It is unsurprising then that caves and places of water, especially springs and lakes, have ancient associations with the Goddess.

Chalice Well is probably the best known sacred water site in Glastonbury, thanks to its links to the Holy Grail but is only one of many sacred springs and wells, some marked, others hidden.

The Goddess's sweet rains pound the lands
torrents off stone
batters the backs of birds
wings splayed, crouched down

falls in gentler showers
to bejewel the whiskers of hare and stoat
slides through briar and bracken
in shining rivulets
drip-feeds fens, bogs and marshes

carves its name upon the land
in mighty rivers
or marks it more gently
all the way to the sea

Between earth and sky
spelled about by Fata Morgana
the lands become as insubstantial as myth

and just as solid

The Goddess mists conceal/reveal
spire, tor and steeple
magic the Isle of Glass into being
and out again

The godmen rebel
take their shovels to the Goddess's river hips
mastectomise Her breasts
confine Her fertile floods with rhynes, canals and channels
sluices, leets, flumes and lades
but godmen come and go
like their temples do
taken by tempests, eaten by damp and dew
the Goddess has many tools
at Her disposal
and Time is on Her side

She goes about Her business underground
rising here and there to gift Her blessings
Red Spring's waters coloured rust
White Spring's waters clear as stars
the Mother Spring, St Mary's in the Crypt
and upwellings less remarked

The godmen search Her flows for blessings too
wine into blood at that last supping
blood collected from the cross
hoarded, hidden, lost and longed for
chalice and grail
myths fractured by fact
and mended by faith

Epilogue

Every now and then, for those of us fortunate to live in comfortable predictability, a disruption occurs. In February 2024, my husband was diagnosed with cancer. We cancelled our plans for the year and began the exhausting journey through medical appointments, tests, hospitals, chemo, and operations. Fear and uncertainty became our travelling companions but also our tools for change.

A comfortably predictable life, as enjoyable as it is, produces stasis rather than growth. It is trauma and testing that produces the change necessary to a more fully realised life. Neither my husband's nor my life were ever going to be the same post diagnosis and although we were both immensely grateful for his successful treatment, I knew I had more to learn from the experience.

So it was, at the end of that year, when my daughter planned a quick trip to London to attend a friend's wedding, I knew it was time to step into a portal (in this instance, a long haul flight) to see what new state I might be delivered to. And when my daughter suggested we add a brief visit to the sacred site of Glastonbury, it seemed more than fitting.

Once back in Australia, I was tempted to reflect on what I had learned in my few days in Glastonbury but sensed that learning (in the usual sense) is of the conscious mind and that Glastonbury, like myth and dream, is of the unconscious. And it seemed to me rather paradoxically, that if anything, I had learned not to learn but to simply accept instead.

Many of us expect a return on our investment of time, expense, and effort expended on travel, and on the mental discomfort the unfamiliar inflicts. It is a return often framed as an expansion of knowledge. We expect to know more about the geography, history, and culture of the places we visit, but sacred spaces are different. What they gift us, if we are open to them, if the time is right, if the chatter of the world is stilled, is a profound deepening.

I have experienced this deepening in other sacred spaces. On the icy deck of a ship off the coast of Norway as auroras plumed the skies; in Purnululu National Park, Western Australia, where the pristine reflections in Cathedral Gorge's pool shone many times brighter than any mirror; and in Outback camps where 360 degree sunsets fill the vast heavenly dome with successive waves of apricot, aqua, powder blue, deep blue and finally, a brilliant star-bedazzled black.

This deepening tells me that beyond the human-conceived gods that come and go, often in bloody entrances and exits, lies something far more enduring. I call it the Goddess in recognition of its creative essence and while it is beyond human grasp or definition, it is not beyond human sensibilities.

So, what exactly, did this deepening in Glastonbury gift me?

In taking a portal away from my normal existence, I was able to accept and celebrate my cronehood by reacquainting myself with the Triple-Form Goddess.

I became less controlled by the peculiar thing we call Time and less concerned about the number of years Time has already measured out for me and how few might be left.

I was able to contemplate the temples' struggles to confine and define the unknowable, and to realise how fragile words are in encapsulating what I came to call the Goddess. I was able to walk the grief-filled grassy paths between graves and the ancient labyrinthine ones that connect us to something far greater than this human life.

And I was able to see afresh the pervasiveness of the Goddess in Her sacred springs and wells, streams and rivers, rains and mists; in Her water into wine and wine into blood, revered in chalice and grail; in Her trinity reimagined in enduring temple stories as the Father, Son and Holy Ghost; in Her timelessness as Isis, Mariam, Mary, and yet always, through Time and place, true to Her own wise, all-knowing, infinite Self.

I hope you enjoyed *Glastonbury - Meditations on the Goddess*. **Authors need reviews!** It is how our readers find us. I would love you to leave an honest review on Amazon, Goodreads, or another of your favourite reader sites. If the inner journey intrigued you, read on.

Works by K S Nikakis

Non Fiction

Journey: Seeking the Sacred, Spirit and Soul in the Australian Wilderness – For fans of Joseph Campbell's hero journey

When we set out into the wilderness, what is it we really seek?

Do we seek new sights or do we seek new selves? And are we really on one journey or on two?

Journeying fifteen thousand kilometres into Australia's blood-red heart, Nikakis discovers that every journey is perilous, for travellers risk carrying the clutter of their outer lives with them; a clutter that blinds them to the other journey they crave; that of the inner soul-journey into a deeper understanding of self.

To enter Australia's vast Outback wilderness, is to enter a place of endless horizons; a place doused with brilliant gold dawns and dazzling sunsets; a place silvered by star-encrusted night skies and, most importantly, a place of hidden sacred places in whose deep stillness our inner journeys can at last unfold.

In the spirit of travellers like Robert Macfarlane and Scott Stillman, Nikakis asks what it is we really see, feel and understand when we follow in the steps of those who have gone before us deep into the wilderness.

Drawing on her Ph.D. in Joseph Campbell's hero myth, and using original poetry and novel extracts, Nikakis takes us on this second journey; a journey of the sacred, spirit and soul, where our inner selves finally have the time and space to gift us richer and more fully-realised lives.

In the Company of Birds - Poems from an Outback Odyssey – For fans of Outback Australia https://www.amazon.com.au/dp/B0CPGZJ1CX

What do we lose when we cease to be a child and become an adult? What precious thing do we let slip away and barely notice?

Watch any child in a garden or park or wilderness area as they discover the natural world. Listen to their ooh's of delight at the sight of a caterpillar on a leaf, their excited squeals as a butterfly bobs past, their clap of hands and gap-toothed grins at the gambol of some young animal.

Children delight in the most common and mundane elements of the natural world with a pure and unsullied joy that many of us, somewhere in our journey to adulthood, have lost. We largely remain unaware of our loss, although I recall the exact moment I became conscious that while I saw the beauty of the natural world, I no longer felt it in the deepest parts of my soul.

As adults, we might continue to admire the natural world's beauty on an intellectual level and seek connection with it for our physical, mental, and spiritual health. It's one of the reasons I set out on a 50 day journey through Australia's southern wilderness, but how often do we ignore the sparrows at our feet in our eagerness to admire the eagles that soar above? And when so many things demand our adult attention, how do we even make time to look in the first place?

Beauty surrounds us, as it surrounds a child, but our adult gaze seeks out the extraordinary and so blinds us to the ordinary, denying us the visceral joy that such things deliver. To reclaim this joy, we must suspend our adult judgement and clear our gaze as a child does.

A journey in the company of birds allows us the time and space to do so. Birds require us to search the ground as well as the sky, to delight in the raven's harsh croak as well as the honeyeater's sweet song, to take pleasure in the sparrow's brown plumage as well as the fairywren's blue. And as we still, and look, and listen, we are ultimately rewarded with the return of all we've lost.

And so, let us begin this journey of rediscovery, in the company of birds.

Fantasy Novel Series

Angel Caste 5 book series
Book 1 Angel Blood

Street-kid, thief, criminal: Viv is desperate to change her life.

On day release from jail to attend the funeral of her father, a violent drunk she feared and despised, her real father turns up, the powerful angel Archae Kald. He offers to reunite Viv with the mother she thought dead and, determined to find the only person who has ever loved her, Viv travels through a rift to the male angel world of Ezam.

Kald assigns his protégé, the beautiful angel Thris, to guide Viv to her mother. It is Thris's job to keep Viv safe in the Rynth, the vast tangle of worlds she never knew existed. But Viv is deeply damaged from her life on the streets and in no mood to trust anyone, even an angel with a face to die for. They set out, but as the complications multiply, disaster follows.

Thris might be eons old, but he knows little about females, especially ones who are half human. Like his closest friends, Ash and Ky, all he wants to do is transcend but when he and Viv stumble into the acrid world of Moth Fold, and Viv's latent angel traits emerge, transcendence seems the last thing possible.

After a devastating attack, Viv ends up lost and alone in the Rynth. Will she survive to continue the search for her mother? Or end her days in an alien world?
If you like your female heroes feisty, your male angels glorious, your fantasy worlds filled with brilliant landscapes

and a dash of romance, you will love *Angel Blood*, Book 1 in the five book fantasy series *Angel Caste*.

Buy *Angel Blood* today to start your amazing adventure with Viv and Thris in the wild worlds of the Rynth.

Book 2 Angel Breath

Viv can survive on the streets, but can she survive in the Rynth?

Thris is gone, his exquisite body torn apart, and borne away by Ash and Ky. Viv fears she will never see him again, but there is no way she is turning back. She journeys on through the Rynth, narrowly escaping murderous landscapes and worlds full of savage creatures. Her life on the streets might have been a nightmare, but at least it taught her how to run, hide, and out-wit pursuers.

And then, when all seems lost, Thris returns. Viv is overjoyed, but her happiness is short-lived. He isn't the angel he was, and he isn't alone. Ky is with him, and Ky hates Viv. The feeling is mutual, but Ky's terror of the Rynth adds to their peril and they don't get far before they are besieged by savage, long-armed creatures. When Ky is injured, Thris is confronted with a terrible decision, and must abandon Viv to save him.

Viv journeys on but stumbles into a war zone. Desperate to escape, she is determined to take the next rift out, but finds a little girl, the sole survivor of a massacre. Recognizing the chance to make amends for the accident that landed her in jail, Viv delays the search for her mother, to take the little girl to safety.

But in an alien, war-torn world, it is all but impossible to tell friend from foe, and when the little girl falls ill, Viv must take a terrible risk. Will Viv manage to save the little girl? Or will the fighting cost them both their lives?

If you like your female heroes feisty, your male angels glorious, your fantasy worlds filled with brilliant landscapes and a dash of romance, you will love *Angel Breath*, Book 2 in the five book fantasy series *Angel Caste*.

Buy *Angel Breath* today to continue your amazing journey with Viv and Thris through the wild worlds of the Rynth.

Book 3 Angel Bone

Viv didn't abscond from jail to become someone else's prisoner, but that seems to be her fate.

As chance would have it, she resembles a people called the elddra, and that makes her both despised and desired. It also makes friends few and far between. Viv is desperate to deliver the little girl to safety, take a rift out, and resume the search for her mother, but dodging the new world's warring factions proves harder than she thinks.

As they journey on through strange and hostile lands, the little girl's trust and affection for Viv grows, and Viv is surprised by her own feelings of fierce protectiveness. And then, as they near safety, disaster strikes. They are overtaken by fighters and separated. Viv is seized and when the fighters are annihilated by a second force, their leader assumes she is one of the enemy. Prevented from executing her on the spot, the leader condemns her to a slower, more painful death.

In his own world, Thris struggles to care for Ky who is traumatized by his time in the Rynth, and when Ky flees, they end up imprisoned in a maze-like world where the only way out is a death-trap. Their hopes for rescue lie in Ash, but Ash is trapped too, entranced by a world of shining light, and unaware of his friends' plight.

Will Viv survive to be reunited with the child she loves? Or will she lose her too, as she has lost her mother and Thris?

If you like your female heroes feisty, your male angels glorious, your fantasy worlds filled with brilliant landscapes and a dash of romance, you will love *Angel Bone*, Book 3 in the five book fantasy series *Angel Caste*.

Buy *Angel Bone* today to continue your amazing journey with Viv and Thris through the wild worlds of the Rynth.

Book 4 Angel Bound

Viv thought things couldn't get any worse, but she is about to be proved wrong.

Disfigured by the ordeal she has somehow managed to survive, she realizes her grotesque appearance prevents her continuing her search for her mother and ends any hope of a future with Thris.

But Viv's angel blood is strong and, aided by its healing, she sets out to find the little girl. She is helped by a man whose kindness is something she has never experienced before, and love blossoms. He demands her trust, but haunted by images of witch-burnings, Viv daren't reveal what she really is. Complications multiply until being with him, and the child she loves, seems all but impossible.

Thris is bound by his pledge to guide Viv to her mother, and returns, but his search for Viv ends so catastrophically, that he yearns for death. All Viv's nightmares come true when she discovers his fate, but saving him, might cost the lives of countless others.

In Thris's absence, Ky and Ash uncover warnings about a trinity of angels the three of them resemble but who disappeared eons before in mysterious circumstances. The warnings about their fate are fragmentary, as if they have been deliberately destroyed.

Can Viv save the angel she loves? Or will she lose him and everything else she has come to care about?

If you like your female heroes feisty, your male angels glorious, your fantasy worlds filled with brilliant landscapes and a dash of romance, you will love *Angel Bound*, Book 4 in the five book fantasy series *Angel Caste*.

Buy *Angel Bound* today to continue your amazing journey with Viv and Thris through the wild worlds of the Rynth.

Book 5 Angel Blessed

It seems Lady Luck has smiled on Viv at last. Or has she?

When Viv is offered the chance of a home with the little girl she loves, she grabs it but then the child is snatched. To rescue her, not only must Viv battle the little girl's enemies, but those who love the child as well.

The perilous quest leaves Viv horribly injured, and she ends up in a world where she is offered the opportunity to finally heal herself. It means opening herself to terrible new risks but also the possibility of securing the little girl's safety, once and for all.

She returns to the child's world but is pursued by those who believe she holds the key to their deepest desires and, as their threats escalate to violence, Thris reappears. Viv's happiness soon turns to dread, as he reveals a threat that could destroy the little girl's world, as well as his own. Thris joins with Ky and Ash in a desperate fight to avoid the impending catastrophe and as events build to a climax, Viv prepares to sacrifice everything for those she loves.

Will Viv's search finally deliver her the loving home she craves? Or will she, and those she cares about, end their lives in the cataclysm that threatens?

If you like your female heroes feisty, your male angels glorious, and your fantasy worlds filled with brilliant landscapes and a dash of romance, you will love *Angel Blessed*, the final book in the five book fantasy series *Angel Caste*.

Buy *Angel Blessed* today to conclude your amazing journey with Viv and Thris through the wild worlds of the Rynth.

Angel Caste – Complete 5 Book Series

A troubled half-angel, a beautiful angel guide, a binding promise . . .

Viv is on day release from jail to attend the funeral of the thug she thinks is her father, when she comes face to face with her real father, the powerful angel Archae Kald. If finding out she's a half-angel isn't shocking enough, Viv discovers her mother isn't dead after all but lost somewhere in the tangle of worlds called the Rynth.

Determined to find the only person who has ever truly loved her, Viv goes to Kald's angel world where he appoints the beautiful Thris as her guide. Thris is kind and caring, unlike the males Viv has known before, but after living on the streets, Viv finds it almost impossible to trust.

Friendship grows as Thris trains her to travel the rifts, but the Rynth is a dark and dangerous place, even for angels and, as Thris grows increasingly tempted by Viv's emerging angel traits, disaster strikes.

Viv journeys on alone and stumbles into a war zone where she finds a lost child. She pledges to take the child to safety but, as the war rages on, deciding who is friend and who is enemy becomes a deadly game of chance.

Bound by his promise to guide Viv to her mother, Thris embarks on a desperate search for her, but a greater threat confronts them both and, in the end, they must fight not just for their own lives, but for the lives of those they love.

The Kira Chronicles - 6 book series
Book 1 The Whisper of Leaves

A gold-eyed Healer, a prophecy, two brothers at war.

In seasons long past, twin gold-eyed princes sundered a kingdom. Rejecting his brother's warrior ways, Kasheron led his people away to establish the Tremen community of Allogrenia, deep in the great southern forests. Forgotten by the outside world and protected by the trackless trees, the Tremen flourish for seasons uncounted, upholding Kasheron's legacy of peace and healing.

All Tremen delight in the healing arts, but Kira is the greatest Healer of them all.

To the north of Allogrenia, drought grips the land, and the Shargh suffer. A herding people, they lost their grazing tracts to the Northern invaders years before, through long and bloody wars. As the drought tightens its grip, and their herd animals die, the chief's younger brother seizes on an ancient prophecy to snatch the chiefship for himself.

The prophecy links the Shargh's doom to a gold-eyed Healer, and Kira has gold eyes.

The Shargh attack with devastating consequences, and Kira must fight to save the wounded. But the Shargh wounds rot, no matter her skill, and as the blood-shed continues, Kira faces losing everything and everyone she loves.

Can Kira cure the Shargh wounds? Or will the Tremen community be destroyed? If you love your female heroes feisty, your fantasy worlds with sun-dappled forests, quiet owl-filled nights, and just the right dash of romance, you will love *The Whisper of Leaves*, Book 1 of the six book *The Kira Chronicles* series.

Buy *The Whisper of Leaves* today to enter the forest world of the Tremen and start your amazing adventure with Kira as she fights to save her people.

Book 2 The Silence of Stone

How can fire quench fire?

The Tremen are dying and Kira is in a deadly race against time to save them. Somewhere deep in the Warens' labyrinth of underground tunnels, lies the answer to a riddle and the cure to Shargh wounds.

To find it, she must defeat the tunnels' unmapped darkness *and* Kest, the blue-eyed, blond-haired Commander of the Protectors. As leader of the force Kasheron established to keep the Tremen safe, Kest is sworn to protect, and everything Kira does puts her at terrible risk.

As she fights to heal, and he to protect, they join in an uneasy alliance to save the people they love.

When Kira is made Tremen Leader, the stakes rise even further. The Tremen are riven by division and Kira must fight to stop the Tremen community from breaking apart. Desperate to find the cause of the Shargh attacks and stop the Tremen's suffering, she goes ever deeper into the Warens' perilous darkness. Kest searches too, his quest in the sunlit forests above.

When he and his men make a gruesome discovery, he realizes what drives the Sharghs' murderous attacks, but then he makes a deadly mistake.

As Kira learns more of her brutal lineage, she is confronted with the horrifying truth that to save her people, she must lose them forever. Can Kira preserve Kasheron's legacy of peace and healing? Or will all he fought for be swept away by the violence he fled?

If you love your female heroes feisty, your fantasy worlds with sun-dappled forests, quiet owl-filled nights, and just the right dash of romance, you will love *The Silence of Stone*, Book 2 of the six book *The Kira Chronicles* series.

Buy *The Silence of Stone* today to enter the forest world of the Tremen and start your amazing adventure with Kira as she fights to save her people.

Book 3 The Secrets of Stars

What truths lie hidden in the stars?

Kira is alone, her food all but exhausted, the forest and those she loves, far behind her. When she stumbles on a stranger under attack, she faces a terrible choice: betray everything Kasheron fought for or walk away.

The stranger, Caledon, knows a path over the mountains and has friends nearby who can help them, but Kira's quest is clear: go straight north, gain aid for her people, and return home.

They continue together but the Azurcades are perilous and when a terrible storm threatens to sweep them to their deaths, their journey becomes a battle for survival.

Kira's trust in Caledon grows and his gentleness rouses other, deeper feelings, but Caledon is ruled by forces that pose a lethal threat to her quest. She plans her escape, but new lands bring new enemies and she is taken prisoner.

Fleeing her captors, Kira finds herself with a people under Shargh attack. As the carnage mounts and she joins with their Healers to save the wounded, her stocks of fireweed run dangerously low. Caledon strives to regain her trust and the stakes escalate when he reveals terrible truths that threaten the Tremen's very existence.

As the slaughter continues and Kira embarks on a hazardous search for fireweed, disaster strikes and she is snatched by the Shargh warrior who has long hunted her. Can Kira survive to reach the north and finally deliver aid to her people? Or will her quest end at the Shargh's brutal hands?

If you love your female heroes feisty, your fantasy worlds with sun-dappled forests, quiet owl-filled nights, and just the right dash of romance, you will love *The Secrets of Stars*, Book 3 of the six book *The Kira Chronicles* series.

Buy *The Secrets of Stars* today to enter the forest world of the Tremen and continue your amazing adventure with Kira as she fights to save her people.

Book 4 The Thunder of Hoofs

Who is friend and who is enemy?

When Kira's Shargh captors are attacked, she finds herself a prisoner of those who might prove even deadlier. But then, in a heart-rending twist of fate, their leader is revealed to be the bearer of everything Kira most loved in the world *and* everything Kasheron most despised.

Kira hides her identity but her subterfuge is discovered and the dangers multiply. Her quest is to gain aid from her northern kin, but the forests that hid the Tremen from enemies, also hid them from friends, and there is no help for a people without alliance or treaty. To make matters worse, the northern histories tell a very different story of the great Healer Kasheron.

To aid the Tremen, Kira must turn south again, to where Caledon will bring the Tremen fighters but she and the northern leader share a powerful attraction and he's determined to keep her safely in the north, far from the Shargh.

Desperate to learn of Kira's fate, Caledon journeys north too and they are reunited, but his arrival generates antagonisms that threaten alliances and treaties alike. As Caledon strives to decipher the stars' intent, the stakes escalate, and he fears following his heart could cause the deaths of countless others.

Kira is no slave to the stars and, driven by her duties as leader, sets out for the south. Besieged by squalling winds and icy storms, her escort comes under Shargh attack and she finds herself in a desperate flight through the night in a terrifying attempt to outrun them. But Shargh hunters lie in wait, and in a deadly rain of spears, her mare goes down. Can Kira survive to finally deliver aid to her people? Or will her quest end in the wind-swept darkness?

If you love your female heroes feisty, your fantasy worlds with sun-dappled forests, quiet owl-filled nights, and just the right dash of romance, you will love *The Thunder of Hoofs*, Book 4 of the six book *The Kira Chronicles* series.

Buy *The Thunder of Hoofs* today to enter the forest world of the Tremen and continue your amazing adventure with Kira as she fights to save her people.

Book 5 The Crying of Birds

Must Tremen healing bow before Terak swords?

Kira's deepest fears are realized when the Tremen are forced from the forests to join the devastating conflict on the plain. To add to her guilt, she can't remain with the people she leads but must go north. Sarnia has no healing, and if the fighting spreads, their wounded will die.

Leaving behind those she loves, she endures the perilous journey back to Sarnia, only to confront powerful forces determined to keep the ways of the despised Healer Kasheron out of the city. As Kira fights to create a place of healing, aid comes from an unexpected quarter, but a healing place without fireweed will save no lives.

Kira's search for fireweed grows increasingly desperate and then her worst nightmare comes true when the person she loves most in the world is mortally wounded. As the fighting drags on and winter deepens, the injured flood in and Kira's struggle to save them takes a deadly toll.

In the south, the Shargh tribes join, and Tierken makes a terrible mistake that puts Sarnia at risk. Distrust weakens their forces and as the bloodshed grows, treachery promises to deliver a Shargh victory. And then, as Tierken and his men fight for their very existence, word reaches him that Kira's life hangs in the balance. Faced with a terrible dilemma, he makes a choice that risks the destruction of his leadership in the north

Kira flees to the healing settlement of Kessom but to reach its sanctuary, she must navigate the raging torrent that claimed

Tierken's father. Will Kira survive to reach the healing she so desperately needs? Or will her journey end in the watery darkness?

If you love your female heroes feisty, your fantasy worlds with sun-dappled forests, quiet owl-filled nights, and just the right dash of romance, you will love *The Crying of Birds*, Book 5 of the six book *The Kira Chronicles* series.

Buy *The Crying of Birds* today to enter the forest world of the Tremen and continue your amazing adventure with Kira as she fights to save her people.

Book 6 The Music of Home

What is the price of peace?

With the fighting over, Tierken pursues Kira to Kessom where she is overjoyed to be reunited with him, but neither have escaped the battles unscathed. Kira's health is fragile and Tierken's aggression is honed from months of fighting. To add to the complications, Tierken's enemies in Sarnia have taken full advantage of his absence in the south.

Angered by their scheming and frustrated by Kira's refusal to bend to his will, his arguments with her escalate until Kira realizes the breach between the Tremen and Terak is too large for her to mend. Her hopes for a future with Tierken shattered, she sets out for home, but the Sarsalin is full of dangers and enemies lie in wait.

Caledon waits too as he struggles to reconcile his own want of Kira with the wants and needs of the stars. They travel south together and when they come upon a sick Shargh child, Kira begins to understand the brutal consequences of the fighting, and that bloodshed can only ever seed more bloodshed.

Desperate to prevent future warfare, Kira resolves to offer the Shargh people healing, despite knowing it will likely cost her life. But when she reaches the Shargh settlement, she makes a shocking discovery that changes everything.

There are Shargh women there who crave peace as she does, but she comes face to face with the man who believes her death will deliver him everything he desires, and as the final chilling part of the last Telling unfolds, she realizes for the first time, what is truly precious to her and what is worth fighting for.

Will Kira survive to return to all she loves, or make the ultimate sacrifice as she strives for peace?

If you love your female heroes feisty, your fantasy worlds with sun-dappled forests, quiet owl-filled nights, and just the right dash of romance, you will love *The Music of Home*, the final installment in *The Kira Chronicles* series.

Buy *The Music of Home* today to enter the forest world of the Tremen and complete your amazing adventure with Kira as she fights to save her people.

The Kira Chronicles – Complete 6 Book Series

A gold-eyed Healer, a prophecy, two brothers at war.

In seasons long past, twin gold-eyed princes sundered a kingdom. Rejecting his brother Terak's warrior ways, Kasheron led his people deep into the great southern forests and established the healing settlement of Allogrenia. The Tremen flourished, upholding Kasheron's legacy of peace and healing, and protected by the vast, trackless trees.

All Tremen delight in the healing arts, but Kira is the greatest Healer of them all.

To the north of Allogrenia, drought ravages the Shargh's land, and as their suffering escalates, the chief's younger brother seizes on an ancient prophecy to snatch the chiefship for himself. The prophecy links the Shargh's doom to a gold-eyed Healer, and Kira has gold eyes.

The Shargh attack with devastating consequences and Kira must fight to save the wounded, but the Shargh wounds rot, no matter her skill, and Kira finds herself in a deadly race against time. As the slaughter continues, she makes the horrifying discovery that the Shargh hunt *her*. To halt the attacks and save her people, she sets off for the North to seek aid from her long sundered warrior kin.

But the dangers beyond the forests exceed even the Shargh attacks. The Tremen detest their warrior kin but Terak's descendants have inflicted a worse fate on the Tremen. Kira's new-found love is torn apart by ancient hostilities and when trust turns to betrayal, it risks everything she has fought for.

As the battles rage on, Kira becomes increasingly sickened by the bloodshed. Desperate to end the suffering once and for all, she sets out on a quest that could cost her everything and everyone she loves.

Fantasy Novels

The Emerald Serpent

Check out the fabulous book trailer:
https://www.youtube.com/watch?v=bGpKxnpCEMg

Betrayal, torture, death: Etaine lives on only to destroy those who robbed her of everything she loved.

Seven years before, Etaine met fellow Ranger Cormac, the he-Eadar she believed was her longed-for true-mate. Emerald-eyed, white-skinned, and black-haired, the Eadar had formed into Ranger bands to fight the Fada, invading religious zealots determined to replace the Eadar's Serpent Goddess with their own gods of stone.

The pure blood of the ancient Eadar runs strong in Etaine and Cormac's veins, and their joining had the potential to open the Emerald and Serpent Ways to them, old worlds only true Eadar can enter. But their love affair goes tragically amiss, with catastrophic consequences.

Etaine flees and as the years pass, slowly rebuilds her life, but the Fada's attacks grow more ferocious, and the Eadar are forced to fight for their very existence. When the Fada mass to commit yet more bloody slaughter, and the bands join in a final, desperate effort to defeat them, Etaine comes under Cormac's command, the very last Eadar she ever wants to see again.

Together they have a weapon that can destroy the Fada, but to use it, Etaine must learn to trust again and Cormac to Remember. And time runs short: the Serpent rises.

Don't miss the enthralling story of Etaine and Cormac's fight to defeat the Fada and revive the old worlds of the Eadar. Set in the ancient Caledonian Forest of Northern Scotland, with its misty crags and bright, rushing streams, *The Emerald Serpent* will delight those who love their fantasy with a touch of Celtic and a dash of romance.

Buy *The Emerald Serpent* today to share Etaine and Cormac's amazing quest to rid their beautiful worlds of the Fada threat.

Heart Hunter

Fleet is a young Sceadu hunter: skilled, strong, and fast. She hunts deep into the icy mountains, seeking meat for her people, for the rains have failed and plunged the Sceaudu into hunger.

Her hunts are hard, but she has much to look forward to. Soon she will be gifted her air-name by the Sceadu's shaman, and then she will be a full adult, and free to marry the man she loves.

But while Fleet is on hunt, the old shaman dies, and the new shaman visions a very different future for her: cross the frozen, ice-locked mountains and complete a perilous quest or lose the man she loves forever.

In a moment of anger and frustration, Fleet commits a terrible wrong and sets out into the frigid mountains to atone with her life. In a journey that takes her deep into the earth's darkest places, into strange new worlds, and even into Death itself, she discovers that only she can save her people. To survive, she must draw on every shred of her hunter strength, and doing the impossible, it turns out, is just the beginning.

If you love strong, independent female hunters, bright snowy landscapes, worlds where truth might lie in the mystical realms of a vision-quest, and a dash of romance, you will love *Heart Hunter*.

Buy *Heart Hunter* today to share Fleet's danger, joy, and discoveries in her quest to save her people and the man she loves.

The Third Moon

Where does the past end and the future begin?

Haunted by inherited memories of his people's dispossession and theft of their children, Warrain is just twelve years old when the nightmare repeats. But Warrain isn't living on Earth in the 21st Century, he is living on the planet Imago in the far flung future.

Five years before, Station One's Mech's got high on the opioid arrash, and in the bloodshed that followed, Warrain's scientific community were expelled from the Station, his father murdered, and his mother and unborn sibling lost to him.

The scientists carve out a rudimentary Station high in Imago's ranges, and Warrain's friends get on with their lives. Not Warrain; he climbs the Tors to stare down at Station One, dream of his mother and sibling, and plot revenge.

And then one day, everything changes. A third moon appears in the sky, one of Imago's life-forms calls him by name, and disease breaks out at Station One.

When the Mechs visit to seek help for their ill, Warrain seizes the opportunity to deal them a blow they will never forget. But the third moon brings changes that threaten them all and, to aid the life-form whose kind is being dispossessed and slaughtered, he must turn his back on the hate that has long sustained him and find another way to live.

If you are fascinated by the power of memory, the excitement of life on other planets, and like your fantasy with a dash of romance, you will love *The Third Moon*.

Buy *The Third Moon* today to share Warrain's life on Imago as he struggles to protect Imago's creatures and make the planet truly his home.

Messenger

In a world made deaf by hatred, who will hear the messenger?

Severine's world ends the day her family is murdered. Being raised in the loving community of gay Travelers always marked her as an outsider, but being female puts her in mortal danger. Women are scarce, precious, and hunted.

When chance brings Severine face to face with the father she has never known, he assigns the son of his murdered best friend to guard her. They soon clash. Severine believes all men are violent brutes and Jeph resents his freedoms being curtailed.

An uneasy understanding grows but Jeph is glad to deliver her to the Enclaves, a sanctuary her father has carved out in the mountains for his women and children. But there is no safety in a world broken by war and sickness and when violence follows her, Severine flees to the northern city of Andhaka in search of a home amongst her mother's people. Jeph follows, bound by loyalty to her father, but the north holds terrible dangers for him.

It's been years since Andhaka has welcomed outsiders with anything but bullets, and to survive and to protect Jeph, Severine must learn to use her enemies' weapons against them. As the stakes rise, she comes to understand the horror of her mother's loss, and what drove her father north seventeen years before. His quest becomes her quest, but she hasn't counted on the savage legacy that war and sickness have left behind, or on falling in love.

Can Severine succeed where her father failed? Or will her fate prove even deadlier than his? If you love your fantasy set in brilliant new worlds, with characters you really care about, and just the right dash of romance, you will love *Messenger*.

Buy *Messenger* today to share Severine's journey as she fights for a home, the man she loves, and a better world.

I Heard the Wolf Call My Name
Finalist Best YA Novel – 2019 Aurealis Awards

Jax is on the run from his past. A shifter from the island of Rua, he is trapped on the mainland amongst the despised Off-islanders. Even worse, he is in the military, with a less than exemplary military record.

So when he is ordered to pack up his kit and is flown away in the middle of the night, he is in no position to argue. And it isn't as if he has any other place to go.

Ten years before, when Jax was just twelve years old and in bird-form high above his island home, it blew to smithereens, leaving him the only survivor, or so he believes.

The mystery flight dumps him at a new base where he comes face to face with Matiu, the boyhood friend Jax thought was as dead as his previous life. The military want Jax for an important mission and Matiu wants Jax too, but for different reasons, but there is no way Jax is going to resurrect what took him ten long years to bury.

As the pressure on him ramps up, Jax flees but is confronted by something more deadly than his nightmarish memories.
To stop the other Islanders suffering the same fate as his people, Jax must finally face who and what he really is and decide where he truly belongs.

Like stories that question what it means to be human? That escape the narrow definitions of friendship and love? If so, you will enjoy Jax and Anahera's journeys.

Buy *I Heard the Wolf Call My Name* to see the world through very different eyes.

Young Adult

The Dragon of the Drowned World

When the earth shivers and shakes and the oceans rise over the lands, thirteen year old Jojo washes up on a strange shore. The adult survivors build a ramshackle settlement from the debris the ocean delivers, and make sense of their predicament by comparing themselves to Noah and his Ark.

But not everyone agrees and all Jojo wants is his family back.

He scours the beach each day looking for things that aren't broken or dirty and stumbles on a strange, silvery plate. When the plate is smashed by an older boy, Jojo stores the pieces in his secret cave, but then odd things start to happen. The ferocious blood crabs give way to him on the beach and when he's attacked by a giant serpent, it suddenly lets him go.

His fellow wash up, Lee, finds a strange, poisoned little creature and friendship grows as they team up to save it. Lee insists the creature is a griffin and Jojo's plate pieces belong to a loong or dragon but Jojo has enough problems without adding mythic creatures to the list.

When Lee's little creature takes to the skies and the adults set out to hunt it down, Jojo and Lee embark on a desperate quest to save it. But as their journey takes them ever deeper into danger and the plates seem to grow in power, Jojo fears the dragon might turn out to be the deadliest creature of them all.

Like adventure stories where mythic animals come alive?
Where characters tackle the really big questions about life?
You'll love *The Dragon of the Drowned World.*

Fantasy Short Stories

The White Stag and Other Stories – With Deep Fantasy Retellings

Take a peek at excerpts from this collection.

Glass-Heart *Finalist Best YA Short Story – 2019 Aurealis Awards*

Geth moved amongst his band, exchanging quiet words while they waited. Some he had fought with since the Tallon's foul ships had first found their shores while others had come later, when the burn of cot and kin had sent them from their valleys.

Hate drove them but hate was no shield against arrow and knife. It was fighting skills that kept them hale, and Geth ensured they had them aplenty. He needed them living, not just for their own sakes and his, but for what would come later. When the Tallon's stain had been scoured away, the destroyed must be rebuilt.

Kyth sat alone and he went to her and gazed about. 'The glass-heart's fled, has it?'

'I sent her to a place of safety. She will come to me when it is over.'

'Safety was what I wanted for you!'

'And what I wanted for Nyar.' Her eyes caught the star-sheen as she looked up at him.

'But you can't always have what you want, can you, Ceannasai?'

The Gift

Thariel sat for a long time, surveying all around her, as if she ate the world that would soon be memory. Then she took the harness from the mare, and with soft words, thanked her and bade her farewell. Her own feet she turned towards the forest, tossing her face-plate aside as she went, so that her hair fell loose to her waist, then she discarded her chest-armour, the sword and dagger, her bow and quiver.

The trees closed in and she came at last to the lake Men call Menios and stood for a while on its shore. An owl cried and a mouse shrieked, and all around her the souls of the newly dead jostled in their journey to the void. She stepped into the water and the new life inside her quivered.

'Fear not, little one,' she whispered, in her own tongue. 'We are going home.'

The Tale of Prince Anura

I should have been happy, for she was beautiful. Dark rivers of curls, skin as white as moonlight on water, breasts softer than spawn, and she loved me well. But her chamber was small, no matter the comfort of her bed, and the old feelings of entrapment rose, as persistent as gas that bubbles from rot below still waters.

I sat at the casement and listened, as I had once loitered near the watery skin of the second world and waited. The moon grew large and small many times, but it came at last, as I knew it would. The soft lament on the night-time air, the song of a soul as confined as mine. It took me a journey of many days through the depths of a massive forest to find her tower.

Stone it was and sheer, and as remote as the third world's glimmer had once been. I sang to her and she answered with sweet melodies of her own and we made love as frogs do, with our voices. And when trust had built, she let down her shining ladder of golden hair.

Dragon Sprite

Genn rocketed straight upwards, not just because she enjoyed seeing the limitless blue sky before her, but because a Waiwin's wing shape made vertical flight harder for them. Orin didn't try to catch her but swept in circles around her, gaining height in an ever-narrowing spiral. It was a clever tactic and one Genn didn't believe he had thought of in the instant she had cleared the trees. He had obviously studied her strategies and developed a plan to counter them *or so he thought.*

Genn waited until the spiral narrowed to *axeel*, the minimum distance a Waiwin must keep from a Velven unless she *accepted* him, then swerved towards him, narrowing the distance between them. Orin's eyes flashed to black, shocked she *had* accepted him, but before he could act, she folded her wings and dropped.

The strength that had driven Orin's pursuit had surged to his wing-tendrils in anticipation of locking them with hers and he would struggle even to stay airborne until it flowed back.

Ghost Stream

It rained that day, a mighty deluge and as I watched the water sweep across the ground I wished I had made the water angry earlier. The rain did not last and the next morning the ground was dry as dust but that night I was woken by a roar. Worse still, was the pound of hoofs that told me the cattle ran in panic. The night was thick as I headed out with the stockmen, Billy by my side, to discover the river I had never seen flow, stormed along in full flood. I rode with the men to save the cattle but the water cut between us so that only Billy was with me as we drove the cattle back.

And then the water divided us too. I heard Billy's shout as I spurred after some breakaways, and then my horse was gone, and I was in the torrent, and the night turned in upon itself.

And now I linger here, dead but not at peace, when all I want is rest.

The White Stag

Tom wiped his shaking hand across his mouth and felt the temperature drop. Colder air settled in the holloway but this was something different and he sensed the start of another mind-tricking episode.

There was certainly nothing natural about the mist that swirled about him or the visitors it brought. At first Tom thought the figure he saw was a poacher with an ill-gotten pheasant slung about his shoulders but then he realised it was the hindmost walker in a line of other walkers. They were skin-clad, their naked backs and legs pale in the silvery light. The men carried small packs and spears, the women hide-wrapped bundles or small children. They went without speaking and then they were gone.

Rite

My memories have got pretty jumbled over the years. Sometimes I think I might've been a stockman who drowned when I chased cattle into a flooded river, refusing to let a mob of dumb-arsed beasts outsmart me, or maybe I was a tradie who wouldn't let a bit of water over the road get in the way of the quickest route home. Maybe I dived into a river I thought was deep, or likely didn't think at all beyond beating my mates in, or maybe I did none of these things. Yet in some weird way, I know I died in water, and that if there *is* more than one of me, we all went into the water and bloody well never came out.

I mightn't know how I ended up here, dead but somehow not dead, and a hell of a long way from anywhere I'd ever been before but I do know exactly where *here* is, thanks to the sign driven into the rock-hard ground. Its metal might be a bit rusty but what it says is still pretty clear to anyone who bothers to read it. The thing that's caught me, like a cat catches a mouse, is called a Quartz Blow, but I call it *the She*. The sign has a whole lot of guff about the chemical reactions that happen when volcanoes decide to fizz and how Quartz Blows are formed, but says nothing about how the She keeps me close.

www.ingramcontent.com/pod-product-compliance
Lightning Source LLC
Chambersburg PA
CBHW070943250626
47159CB00009B/3360